THE
JOURNEY OF
DECEIT

THE
JOURNEY OF
DECEIT

A story of treachery in friendship

ANUBHA SAGAR

PARTRIDGE

A Penguin Random House Company

To order additional copies of this book, contact
Partridge India
000 800 10062 62
orders.india@partridgepublishing.com

www.partridgepublishing.com/india

Dedicated to my younger brother Ujjwal, my father and mother who have been an immense source of support and inspiration to me

CHAPTER 1
THE BEGINNING OF IT ALL

"C'mon Jazz, you know that's not possible!" "Everything's possible, Ryan". Jazz and I were sitting in the attic of the rented house. Jazz had challenged me to go on a journey to the most deep and puzzling caves of the world; the Dungeon caves. Every year there were reports of people lost in the Dungeon caves.

Thus, whenever I heard the name of the 'Dungeon caves', a chill always ran down my spine.

I had got lost in my thoughts of fright, when suddenly Jazz clicked his fingers in front of me. He said, "Where are you lost buddy?" I replied, "Aw, nothing. I was just thinking of something".

Soon, we decided to go to bed. All night long, I had absurd dreams. I couldn't figure out a single thing. But one thing was certain, Jazz was being seen in my dreams again and again and was giving a wicked smile, as though he had something evil in mind. The next morning when I woke up, Jazz's first question to me was: "Are you ready with your luggage?" I asked him as to what the matter was. He made me recall our conversation of the previous night.

I said, "Jazz, what is the matter? We did not have an agreement on the topic." Jazz burst with anger. He brought out his revolver and kept it on the side of my forehead just about 2 centimeters above my ear. "Just stop your non sense! Not one more word! You will go, and no discussions beyond that!" Then, he caught hold of my chin and shook my head hard. Suddenly, his cell phone started ringing. He picked it up and looked at me, my arm grasped by his clammy palm. "Listen, my friend Ryan is coming to the Dungeons and I want you to be his guide", said he in a voice, which I had never heard before. I stood there, unable to understand what was happening. My thoughts were clouded, and my body was unresponsive.

I remembered my dreams and Jazz's deceitful smile. My brain felt to be working more than ever and I was getting a severe headache. Blood was gushing through my body at the speed of light, trying to reach every nook and corner of my body, to keep me from passing out. I was sweating and getting tensed. I never knew that the Dungeon Caves would give me such a shock. It was all like déjà vu . . . the dream and what Jazz did. I lost contact with my surroundings and fell onto the ground.

CHAPTER 2
INSIDE THE CAVE

When I woke up, I found myself in a very dark cave. Suddenly, I heard faint noises of people talking. I got my boots on and rushed to the spot, but before I could reach the place, someone just shut the opening.

Though, the opening was shut, still I could hear some voices. "Ha! Now we have enough of them, don't we?" said one voice. "No, not yet, some others have to sacrifice their lives too," said another voice. In no time did I realize that I had been deceived by my friend. I decided to walk down the cave and find a way out of the ghostly place. The atmosphere was dull and dingy and I was feeling as though I had been sent to the bowels of the Earth. At that point of time, I could actually make out as to why the place had been given such a horrendous name. I wondered about all the other people who had come here and never returned. My only possession was my travel back pack. I took out my pedometer and attached it to my foot, to note the distance. I think Jazz had just picked up my bag and left it with me in this cave.

I feel many days must have passed by and I had still not found an exit from the cave. I had a few chocolates to munch on, and two bottles of water, which I was miser with. Being a geologist, I saw and observed the structure of the cave. I had been on various expeditions and excursions to many parts of the world, and had seen numerous kinds of caves and their structures. But this was something completely new to me. The Dungeon Caves were unexplored, since they were said to be extremely dangerous and according to some books, the life in here was unpredictable and despicable.

Although I was surrounded by airs of trouble everywhere, yet I felt that I was indeed fortunate of having got the opportunity to explore the caves which were regarded to be the most treacherous

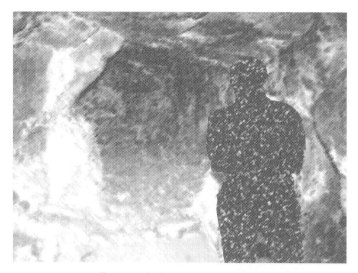

***It was pitch dark as my steps
approached the belly of the cave***

and filled with mythical creatures. I guess the 'mythical creatures' came into virtual existence in the mind of geologists and experts, since not a single person who had gone to the Dungeons had ever returned.

It was pitch dark as my steps approached the belly of the cave. I had an LED torch to guide me, which was slowly discharging. There were some signs of life in there, namely algae and some insects whose names were either not stored in my brain, or my brain was too busy to recall them. All of a sudden, I found something which was familiar; indeed very familiar . . . a human skeleton. This got me all the more anxious. I turned into a bundle of nerves. I had never thought about this in my life, but this sight had compelled me to . . . 'Was I also destined to die here in the Dungeons? Will someone like me come here one day and see my skeleton and wonder the same? Am I soon to die?' The thought of Jazz struck my mind at that moment and I murmured to myself, "Jazz, if I ever meet you again in my life, provided I survive, you shall be my most familiar enemy."

As I walked ahead, I started feeling fatigued and restless. For me, the Earth was rotating faster than ever. Finally, I decided to lie down on the coarse path of the slimy, rock-strewn cave. I rested for a while down there. After that sleep, my memory was absolutely nil, for possibly a few days.

Today, my psychiatrist tells me, that for a while inside the cave, I had gone into fugue.

'Fugue' is a mental disorder that results from an unexpected and unplanned travel. Such a travel contributes to stress and leads to fugue. This disorder had affected me and I had attained a completely new identity. Fugue is a mental state when a person forgets his real identity for a while and this 'while' can be a few hours, days, months and even years. When the memory of the person returns, he or she cannot recall anything from the fugue state.

Fugue affected a portion of my memory for that period, the loss of which is permanent. But, I had a compact voice recorder, which had a major portion of my fugue state in it. As I assume, I must've woken up from sleep and seen the environment around me. I must've noticed my bag lying down on the ground and I must've picked it up, to open it. After having emptied out everything, I must've seen the voice recorder. Out of curiosity, I must've pulled out the voice recorder, switched it on and then started recording my voice.

Here is what I had recorded:

"I-I'm Sa—Sam Groff. I don't know where I'm exactly located, but it seems like a really dark cave. I'm standing on something which looks like a puddle with muck. I'm walking through the weird lanes of this cave. The lanes seem to form a puzzle. I get out of one lane and land up in another! They seem to be leading nowhere.

I'm also getting hunger pangs. The pangs are getting worse every hour. I've been working as a journalist, for a local newspaper in my town. I also have a separate column as an automobile advisor, in the Sunday edition of the newspaper. I strongly feel that, whenever I will get out of this place, I must write about my findings in this cave. This will surely get me fame across the world.

Oh! What do I see here? It seems like a minute insect. I've never seen such an insect before. Maybe it is endemic to this cave. I think I should write about this insect and publish my story in the newspaper. This will get me some fame. Oh, and let me take a picture of this strange creature."

I still have the photo of that insect with me, though I've not been able to figure out what it exactly was. I must've used my camera lying in my bag to take a picture.

"Very well! Now I think that I should move on. Whoa! I see an illusion of my favorite actor on the cave wall! This is amazing. Oh wait, it's not an illusion of my favorite actor . . . it's a cave painting. Now, this is interesting, this painting seems to be very, very old. An ancient painting resembles a present human being's face . . . interesting. I must take a picture of this too. Writing an article on this painting will be fun.

Well, I guess, now I should sleep. I'm so very tired."

This was the end of my recording. Because, after that I was no longer 'Sam Groff'; my memory had returned. Fugue is one amazing disorder. People come back to their normal identity on their own.

Well, I also have Sam Groff's favorite actor's illusion picture, but I don't think I should be wasting my time writing an article about it.

How had my memory returned? Well, it was the same way in which I had turned into Sam Groff earlier. When I had fallen asleep, I think Ryan 'overpowered' Sam Groff and I was normal once again when I woke up.

Today, I know that I had been in fugue. But at that time, I didn't know what I had been doing for the past few hours. For me, I had just woken up from a long slumber.

I continued with my journey. From my last diary entry, it had been more than fifteen days then, since the time I was trying to find an exit from the terrible place.

Suddenly, I happened to chance upon a stream of water. It was crystal clear and the water from it appeared fresh. I cupped my hands and filled them with a bit of water. It was indeed very fresh. All the more, I also saw pieces of coal in the bed of the stream. No wonder the water was so fresh. In electric water filters, carbon is used to remove organic impurities and unwanted odor. There, the coal was being the source of carbon and was making the water clean for drinking. I dipped my hand in and picked up a medium sized block of coal. It was very hard and lustrous. It seemed like Anthracite, the highest rank of coal, in the grading of coal.

Anthracite is mostly used for domestic heating. Lignite ranks lowest in coal grading and is easily available. Bituminous coal is a better quality of coal and ranks one step above lignite. It is mostly used for the production of 'coke', a fuel which is dry and solid. Graphite and Diamond are the purest forms of carbon found in nature. Graphite cannot be kindled easily and is used for making the 'lead' of a pencil. So, the lead of a pencil is not the element 'Lead' which is mentioned in the periodic table as Pb (Plumbum). It is graphite which is the 'lead' of a pencil.

I had examined the coal closely, yet I felt that there was something more to it. Then, just out of the blue, a thought struck my mind. Presence of coal in there was also an indicator for the presence of diamonds. My instinct continuously said to me that there were diamonds in there. Digging deep with dedication could be worth a fortune! I took out my camera and took some snapshots of the coal blocks. This was quite relatable to the diamonds which were found in Kimberley in South Africa. The difference was that they were found on a farm and later that place was converted into a mine. Here it was a natural network of caves with coal and possibly diamonds.

As I moved ahead, I came upon a site which startled me completely. I saw a little pebble, pure white with well-defined edges. I picked it up and scratched the glass of my watch. The glass easily got scratched and broke into two! Thus, the pebble was indeed a diamond.

The find of the diamond was an evidence of the wealth of the cave. My hunch was confirmed.

By then, I was really tired. So I decided to record my findings in my diary, and then rest for a while. As I had been noting the distance that I had covered, I found that I had come two hundred and seventy nine kilometers from the starting. No one knew the correct dimensions of the cave, but according to some approximations, it was said to be around two hundred and eighty three kilometers, along with numerous branching networks with blind ends. A lot of lanes were shut because of heavy boulders.

At that point of time I didn't know if I had taken the correct route. Because, if I had taken a wrong turn I would never find my way out. So, I wasn't really far from the exit. But, to be honest, I had lost all hope of exit from the cave. The journey had been very tiresome and I was getting restless.

I found a stool shaped rock and decided that I would sit there and jot down some findings in the diary. The moment I sat down, the stool sunk down in a weird way and I heard a siren. Something like an arrow pierced my back and inoculated a fluid into my body. I fainted on the spot.

CHAPTER 3
THE VERACITY

When I came back to my senses, I found myself on a strange island. I didn't know how I got there, but I felt much better. I felt extremely relieved after coming out of that deadly cave after approximately eighteen days. It had been a long journey for me and I felt as though heaven had come to my rescue.

But, I was mistaken. Surprise was waiting to happen. Abruptly, four men came and caught hold of me and dragged me to a place, totally unknown to me. When I was being dragged, I was not totally in my senses, but could hear faint voices. I was drowsy, yet, I saw many people working in groups. At some places, the island was quite crammed up with people and there was hardly any space for even two persons to walk. The people were wearing some kind of a turquoise colored uniform with red badges. They were carrying many packets, or rather, sacks on their backs. The sight of the people and the surroundings was pitiable. The people were being hit with whips now and then. There were few children around too, in rags. Those children were either sobbing quietly or wailing loudly. I was almost in tears when I saw them. I'm quite emotional and philosophical by nature. It's sad that people don't understand the plight of laborers. They're treated like slaves. They're not slaves; they never were.

Referring to me, one person said, "Poor person! Now, even he'll have to bear the torture." Soon, the men threw me in a prison and one of them said in a sharp tone, "Hey, you better not try to act smart! Because if you do, then we'll outsmart you! Ha! Anyway, from now on, this is the place where you will live. And yeah, about the work . . . don't worry, it's something you will learn from the people around you!" And after saying this, they went away.

**I felt extremely relieved after coming out of that
deadly cave after approximately eighteen days**

Now, I was completely alone. Though there
were many people around me, I felt alone,
abandoned, and not of great importance. Since
I didn't have much to do, I wondered about the
manner in which I had been brought there. I
remembered the stool which I had sat on. What an
unlucky fate I had! While I was in the cave, I had
seen many such stools on my way. The first stool I
had noticed was when I had covered two hundred
and fifty meters of the cave. Also, many lanes of the
cave had been shut by placing heavy boulders.

Then, I understood the plan which had been made cunningly. The lanes had been shut so that the captive would follow a certain route. The cave was to end at two hundred and eighty three kilometers, so the stool shaped rocks were placed after two hundred and fifty meters. Whenever the person would feel tired, he or she would want to sit on the stools. The stool would sink in and then the alarm would sound. This was to be followed by the injection. The siren must have had a connection with some computer which alerted the person in-charge about the successful inoculation. The person would then be brought to the island by the officials who were in-charge.

My thoughts had got my mind tired and soon, I fell asleep. I dreamt of a beautiful place with all sorts of facilities around. And then, there came a disaster. I was being separated from all the joys. And not much time had passed by, that soon a person came and started whistling. Very soon I realized that it was not the sound of a whistle in my dream, but in reality.

I woke up with a gasp. An angry man came and unlocked the prison. Then, he made me wear the same uniform as the others and commanded me with a shout, to go and start working with the other people. I was shocked. They made me and the other people work hard and with great vim. Initially, I was given the task of cleaning and disinfecting food items, like vegetables and lentils. But slowly, I got to know that the people were into smuggling. The food items were directly imported from the granaries and fisheries. Then, they were brought to the island and drugs were put in them. These food items were later sent back to the cities and villages, where they were sold in the market as regular food. Those drugs were very addictive and so, the people developed an impression that those particular food items had something that attracted them. They were completely unaware of the truth.

I was unwilling to do the horrendous task of putting drugs into the food items, but had no other choice. It made me feel guilty. I had always been against smuggling and all such illegal activities, but there, I was working against my conscience.

While I used to work there every day, I got to know that there weren't only laborers working; software engineers, bankers, doctors and other geologists had also been brought there. They all seemed much stressed out with their jobs. I had tried questioning those software engineers, bankers, geologists and doctors about their work on the island, but all of them gave me a dry response. They hesitated and started sweating if I ever tried to befriend them. I couldn't make out as to why they behaved in such a peculiar manner. They seemed like broken personalities and their morale seemed to have been crushed.

Finally, I couldn't tolerate their silence. I knew that I had to get out of that place and would go to any limits to unravel the truth. I knew that there was something fishy going on.

CHAPTER 4

THE INVESTIGATION

All the people who were into the task of carrying food items to and from the port, putting the drugs into the food items and domestic help were classified under one category: The "Worker association". I was put into the "Technical and Advanced Profession" category, since I was a geologist. All the software engineers, doctors and geologists were in this category. The third category was that of the "Head and Supreme Advisors". The head of the smuggling business, supervisors and advisors were put into this category. The fourth category, "The Protection Squad" consisted of all the guards and constables, who were to protect the area. The last category was that of the "Chefs and Helper Chefs", whose job was to cook and provide meals to all other categories of people. The people from the worker association were rather friendly and open in the way they communicated. I had learned from these workers that the people from all other categories were cold fish. They resisted any sort of friendship and unity.

The next morning I went to one of the so-called constables and asked him, as to where exactly the boss stayed and who he was. The constable hesitated a bit, but then he said, that it was Mr. Jazz Loner.

I couldn't believe my ears. But I tried to show my most normal face and acted natural. I decided that, I would go to the main office building at night and sneak in to find out some important secrets. I asked the constable for more facts and surprisingly he told everything to me. He even told me about his forcible recruitment and about his desperate wish to get out of the dreaded place. He also spilled the beans about the people on important positions in the smuggling business and told me that some of the people who were working were wet behind the ears. He advised me to stay away from the aged workers, since they were more likely to be pessimistic and would not give in to the notion of freedom, because they had lost all hope of liberty.

At night, I went to the main office building. The building wasn't very high, but was tall enough to give a head injury, if someone jumped off. I had a rope which had an iron anchor attached to one end, which could grip the wall edge easily. Using it, I could easily climb up. But before I could do that, I had to cross the security. Obviously, I couldn't enter through the main gate, so I resorted to jumping over the eleven feet high fence. It was a wired fence and could've hurt me badly, if I wasn't cautious. So, very carefully, I put my foldable ladder against the fence, climbed up and sat down on the plain, narrow plank of wood fixed on top of the fence. I pulled the ladder up and lowered it down to the other side of the fence. Slowly, I got down, folded the ladder, kept it in my bag and started walking.

In no time I reached the building. I threw my rope above and fortunately the anchor got the hold on the terrace. Just below the building's terrace was a window. I pulled the rope to check for any

Obviously, I couldn't enter through the main gate, so I resorted to jumping over the eleven feet high fence.

faltering in the anchor. There was none. I went up the rope and then, down to the window. I had picked up the diamond which I had found in the cave. I took it out and scratched the glass of the window. It broke into two. I took both the glass panes and kept them in my bag. To my surprise, there was another glass window. This one was a sliding window, though it was locked. I took out a safety pin from my travel tool case and inserted it into the keyhole. I twisted the safety pin and succeeded in unlocking the window. I jumped inside the room. To my utter astonishment; I found that I was in Jazz's secretary's room. I saw the desk and the file cabinet. I had a strong feeling . . . the file cabinet and the desk held all the secrets of Jazz. I went and pulled out the drawers of the desk, one by one. I couldn't find any files much of use. I approached the file cabinet. Again, I opened all the drawers. In one of the drawers of the huge file cabinet, I found a file with a tag 'confidential'.

In one of the drawers of the huge file cabinet,
I found a file with a tag 'confidential'

Very quickly, I took out my torch light and unzipped the file. Putting the torch light on the paper, I murmured to myself. 'Oil rig set up agreement . . . mm . . . I, Jazz Loner hereby agree to pay fifteen hundred million dollars to Mr. Rupert K. for buying the oil rig.' I turned the page. There was another agreement there. 'Dungeon Caves agreement . . . I Jazz Loner, hereby agree to start a joint business with Mrs. Jane K., w/o Mr. Rupert K., for the extraction of coal and diamonds from the Dungeon Caves.'

Their plan became somewhat clear to me. What they had in mind was to set up an oil rig in the sea and also, to set up a mine in the Dungeon Caves. But, I knew that all of it was illegal.

I zipped the file again and kept it back in the file cabinet. While sliding the drawer back inside the file cabinet, I came upon a photograph of Jazz and a couple standing beside him. The couple seemed outstandingly affluent. I turned the photo. The words 'Jazz Loner and Ks' were scribbled in messy handwriting with a marker. So, it was clear that the 'K couple' was rich and thus, they had made a deal with Jazz.

Taking my bag, I slid the window and went down the rope. Once I reached the ground, I pulled off the rope from the wall, kept it in the bag and took out my foldable ladder. I had taken care to lock the window using the safety pin. Hadn't I done that, there would've been a chaos on the island. Someone would surely have noticed it and complained about it. Also, I had cut the glass pane. I carefully fixed the glass back into place with super glue, which I had managed from my workplace. Though the glass was back in place, the fixed portion was clearly visible. It was all in the hands of God, to keep me safe that night and after that.

I began walking towards the fence. I placed the ladder against the fence and climbed up. Once again, I sat on the narrow wooden plank, took the ladder and put it on the other side of the fence and went down.

What I didn't realize was that, by having done all that sneaking, I had actually honed my skills. After all, everything happens for a reason. And truly, I didn't feel the least guilty about having had a look at someone's confidential documents. Those documents had destroyed so many people's lives. And my life was on the verge of getting destroyed.

I walked towards the rooms. People of all categories had been provided with rooms to stay in, though some of those rooms were in pathetic conditions. The rooms for the "Worker association" were in the worst conditions. The doors were partially broken and made creaking sounds. The ceiling was cracked in some places and water dripped from those cracks, all day long. In the corners of the rooms, algal blooms had come up. Bed bugs and house flies dominated the rooms. The rooms were in a state of complete filth.

The rooms for the people of the Technical and Advanced Profession category were in a better condition. They had almost everything functioning, except for the water supply. Water had to be used very judiciously because; it had a fixed time of supply. It came at seven in the morning and stopped at half past twelve in the afternoon.

And as it was expected, the rooms for the supervisors and advisors were luxurious. No flaw was present and repairs were carried out off and on. The chefs and their helpers were also treated well, since they were the 'food providers'. Their rooms were very clean and tidy and didn't really have any problems of water either.

That night I tried my best to sleep, but couldn't, as I was left wondering as to why the smuggling was going on. If Jazz had to buy the oil rig and do the business with the 'K couple', why would he smuggle?

For the next few days, I kept thinking. My brain seemed to have stopped working and I just did not want to do anything. I observed whatever was going on around me. The people who worked had so many difficulties. They didn't even have time for their kids. But yes, during nighttime, they bonded with their families. I saw the light in their rooms and heard the cheerful noises made by the children. All these human bonds reminded me of my life before Jazz deceived me. Jazz and I had been really good friends. I had known him from the time of elementary school. He had always been somewhat secretive, but I had never let his secrecy come in between our friendship. But what he did was a severe blow to my mind. I tried to run away from the truth but could not.

I remembered all those days I had spent with my family space; those happy moments with my parents and the quarrelsome ones with my sister, Anna Beth. The Sunday evening picnics at the countryside were my favorite. Some time away from the hustle-bustle of the city was a boon. The warm wooden benches of the Church were stress relieving. I have always loved being in the company of God. During winters, the sunlight used to sift through the ground glass windows of the church and the warmth of the sun rays flowed through the large hall where the Sunday mass took place. The high walls of the Church had made me want to stay in the company of God for as long as I could be.

I had also travelled to many places, during my excursions. One of the places whose beauty struck me was Ladakh, in India. Ladakh is a gift of nature. It was surrounded by mountains and hills all around, though all of them were mostly barren. During winters, it was mostly covered in snow. When I came back to my hometown, I had frostbites in my toes. Ladakh was indeed very cold. I had even stood right on the frozen Indus river. A place called 'Draupadi Kund' in Ladakh was something I had never seen before. Draupadi Kund is a pond near Drass (the second coldest inhabited place in the world, after Vladivostok, Russia) which never freezes; no matter how cold the temperature gets. It is said that during the period of exile of the Pandava princes (in the Hindu Religion epic- The Mahabharata), Arjun the Prince Warrior, shot an arrow into the ground to release water, so that his wife Draupadi could take a bath. Scientifically, it is said to be a hot water spring in the depths, hence it never freezes. During summers, only the areas in the vicinity of the rivers became lush green. Those areas had a narrow belt of trees, amidst a surrounding of dry high mountains. The hills in Kargil, a place in Ladakh, seemed to be dotted with shrubs and bushes. That site was mesmerizing.

**Ladakh is a high altitude area, dotted with
dry mountains with snow capped peaks and
a severe, bone chilling cold climate.**

I recall that once I had been to a Buddhist
monastery in Ladakh. The monastery was very
peaceful and quiet. The Lamas were absolutely
detached from the worldly luxuries. Everything
around seemed to be flowing in a disciplined
manner. During my stay at Ladakh, I used to
venture on long treks for hours together, albeit
slowly due to the rare oxygen in the atmosphere
at those altitudes of twelve thousand to fifteen
thousand feet. It was during one such walk that I
saw few large rocks studded with possibly semi
precious stones and gems. At first, I had wanted

to take out the stones and keep them with me, but later I thought that whenever I'll die, I won't be able to take any wealth with me to the other world. And if I took the wealth for contentment till I was alive, I would only increase greed in humanity. So I had left it where it was. I felt that I had done a 'David Livingstone act' just as the famous explorer did on seeing diamonds and alluvial gold , few hundred years ago during his travels from South Africa upwards to then Rhodesia (now Zambia and Zimbabwe) and Tanganika (now Tanzania) . The basic law of nature had come to my mind at that point of time: 'Energy can neither be created, nor destroyed.'

CHAPTER 5

THE REVELATION OF SECRETS

My thoughts had taken a toll on my mind. Finally, I came back on track and decided that from then on I would start my job of attaining liberty. I took out my diary and wrote down whatever I had seen happening around me.

Here is what I had written:

1. *Head of smuggling: Jazz Loner*
2. *Agreements:*
   a. *The Dungeon Caves agreement for diamonds and coal.*
   b. *Oil rig set up agreement*
3. *Smuggling going on.*
4. *Question arises: Why is smuggling going on?*
5. *Other people involved: The 'K' couple (Rupert K. and Jane K.)*

I thought hard and finally figured out what exactly the plan was. Jazz needed money to set up the oil rig and also to set up the mine in the Dungeon Caves. He was smuggling so he could get money and move ahead with his plan. The following day, I went to Peter, one of the computer engineers who were present there. I enquired about his job on the island. I assured him that whatever he told me would not be circulated around. He started fidgeting and I had to calm him down. Finally he spoke up.

'Okay, so I'm Peter, a computer engineer and one of Jazz's colleagues. I was unable to get a job after my graduation and thus, I was incapable of managing my expenses. I thought that Jazz would be able to help me, so I contacted him. When I told my problem to him, he sounded overjoyed. I was annoyed at that but then he said to me that, he had the 'perfect job' for me. When I met him, he told me about this place and the many profits I would make if I worked here. And then, he sent me to the Dungeon Caves by deceiving me. I reached here after many days. When I reached here, I saw that many people were working here as slaves. I was told to be with Wendy and Aryan, who are software and computer engineers respectively. Both Wendy and Aryan are friendly but initially, they were kind of hostile. Today, my job is to create a special program which can store files of all types. Files having extensions of all sorts should be compatible with that program.'

I asked him 'What do you plan to use that program for? I mean explain the program in detail.' When I looked at him, his face was flushed with anxiety. He called Wendy and Aryan. The trio looked kind of nervous. Peter whispered something into Aryan's ear. He seemed shocked. He nodded his head in disagreement and whispered something into Wendy's ear. She too seemed stunned. Finally I lost my patience. I blurted out 'Will someone tell me what's going on in here which is such a big secret?'

At last, Wendy spoke up. 'Well, I'm Wendy, a software engineer. I think that you are the first person to be so interested in our work. Okay, so as you must know, Jazz Loner is involved in smuggling. And we are computer and software engineers. Jazz has assigned to us, the task of creating a private internet system which will be secured with a password. This private internet system, PIST for short, will be used by the high end officials, other smugglers who are involved with Jazz and of course, Jazz himself. PIST will enable Jazz to communicate in ease, with his business partners and others involved with him. We have also been given the task of creating a clandestine banking system online, so that Jazz can establish a parallel banking and currency system'.

I was surprised when Wendy uttered the words 'Parallel Banking'. I said, 'Parallel banking, did you say? Do you mean something like *Bitcoin*?'

Bitcoin was a method of banking in which there was no unified bank power. It was controlled and operated by a certain network. Bitcoins could be purchased through online payment via any currency. Thereafter bitcoins could be used as a virtual currency universally across all countries via the online platform. The money was credited at a fast pace and could be used instantaneously.

These bitcoins could be used for currency trading also. People could get bitcoins by a process called 'mining'. Those bitcoins could not be redeemed as money in metal or any other hard form. It was all based on software. Also, when paying in bitcoins, transactions once made could not be reverted. But one day, the operators of *Bitcoin* shut down the entire system. As a result, all the accounts were closed down. Since people had invested in the virtual money in Bitcoin, they lost all of it. It was a complete scam.

Wendy said, 'Yes, you can say so. This system of parallel banking will be somewhat akin to *Bitcoin*. But, as you can expect, this system is again going to be used for unlawful purposes.'

At last, Aryan drew up the guts and said 'And not to forget, we are also working on a program which will be installed in a special device. This device will enable Jazz to be safe from the police and also any spy agencies who try to sneak in and find out what's going on out here'.

A device? I asked them to give me some more details of the device. But Wendy clearly denied my request. 'Sorry Ryan, it is confidential. We can't let out details any further than these. To be honest, you are the first person who knows what we software and computer experts are up to. I'm really sorry about the inconvenience'. I begged the trio for the details. Aryan said, 'Okay Ryan. Since you are doing the noble task of freeing all of us from this racket, we shall tell you. But, you have to promise us that under no circumstances, should we fall into danger'. I was taken aback by this statement. If these people wanted freedom, they had to take a risk. Yet, I gave my word to them.

Peter said, 'This device called '*Eye On*' will be a very small, wireless machine. It will not even be the size of the nail of the little finger. *Eye On* will be installed in various locations on the island; trees, rocks, all rooms on the island and of course the main building. A small red light will be fixed in it. This light will flicker each time there is a danger. The device will have a program which will know the different types of dangers it has to alert about. This program is termed as 'Smart Protection'. The device shall have a self-camera which will enable

Eye On to 'see' in a way. This camera will be paired with Smart Protection. Thus, Smart Protection controls the camera. Smart Protection will have the different dangers signs installed in it. If a danger will be spotted by the camera controlled by Smart Protection, this Smart Protection will send a signal to the red light, to start flickering. This flicker will be accompanied by an infrasonic siren. The flicker and siren will be low for humans, but strong enough to be sensed by the towers around. These towers will then direct this siren and flicker to the computers in the main building. These computers will then give a loud siren and the word 'Danger' will flash on the screens. The guards and Protection Squad will be sent to the coast immediately and action will be taken according to who the enemy is. The recordings sent to the main computers will be of rather serious nature. Apart from this, if the danger is not much, like a small tussle or something similar, *Eye On* will simply record the happening and send it to our computers within minutes. We'll review the recording and if we find something of serious nature, we'll forward it to the main computers'.

Wendy added, 'But we do all this work so unwillingly'.

I replied, 'Unwillingly for sure. But we have to keep up hope in all spheres of life. Okay, so what all or who all are identified as dangers by *Eye on*?'

Aryan replied, 'Well, as you know, whoever works here has to undergo a procedure that records his or her data. Facial recognition, fingerprint recognition and retina recognition take place before anyone is employed here. So the data of all people working here will be installed in *Eye On*. If the face of a person is not recognized, then it will alert danger. If a person whose fingerprint is not recognized by the main database, he or she is obviously a stranger. So, if such a person happens to touch *Eye On*, it will alert danger. Other people, who are recognized as dangers, are the people of the police force. Smart Protection recognizes these people by their uniforms.'

I remembered that I too had undergone the recognition process. So, even I would be recognized by *Eye On*.

I was surprised. Jazz had kept all sorts of security and safety measures. Also, he had plans of parallel banking ready to escalate the smuggling process. This would in turn get him the money to fulfill his other ambitions.

I thanked them and proceeded towards the doctor's room. Being the only doctor present there, he remained aloof from everyone else. I spoke to him and got to know that he was mainly working for taking care of all categories of people except the Worker Association. He said, 'The people of the Worker Association have very few rights. But still, they come to me and ask for help. Although it is against my contract to take care of them, yet being a doctor, my conscience doesn't allow me to deny them the healthcare. I have to take care of patients, because that is what my profession demands.'

As far as my work was concerned, the other geologists and I were not really involved in heavy load of work. Usually, we used to just roam on the island looking at the misery and wretchedness of the people. The other geologists had told me that we would be working properly when the 'time' came.

But I had decided not to let the 'time' come. I wanted to end this racket as soon as possible. I had found out from some more sources that some of the food which was loaded with drugs was taken down midway. The drugs were then taken out. They were then sold raw in the local market, of course, secretly.

At last I was ready with my plan. I decided that this would be it. Nobody could save this racket.

CHAPTER 6
WHAT'S WITH THIS EYE ON?

For some days, I collected more information. After about two weeks, I had made up my mind and was ready to execute the plan. Since I couldn't have done everything on my own, I needed a team. I approached the people of the worker association. They were quite excited and readily agreed to my plan. The constable was right in telling me about the pessimism of the aged workers. I had tried speaking to them, but they plainly refused.

Apart from this, I had told Wendy, Aryan and Peter to continue with their work. But the twist was that they had to give the password of the PIST to me. Therefore, I would be in control of the entire system. I had assured the trio that if there would be any problem, I would be their safeguard. The doctor, James Freeman, was hesitant to give in to my idea of the plan, but at last he agreed. The other geologists, Graham and Emily were interested in my plan since the time I had told them about my amazing find in the Dungeon Caves. They had said to me that I was 'The person with a plan'. They found me to be quite a workaholic when I told them about my various expeditions. I was quite delighted to hear that, since I had always thought that other people worked more than I did.

Wendy, Peter and Aryan had also given a special name to me. They called me as 'Lodestar'. They took me to be an inspiration and had entrusted their faith in me completely.

In the next few days, I saw something being set up in the sea. I took my binoculars and glared right at the sea. Huge cranes were lowering down some machines into the sea. I got dressed in proper gear and went down to the sea. I hid behind one of the coconut trees. I took my binoculars again and looked straight. I couldn't believe what I saw. Jazz had already started setting up the oil rig! Those machines were going to be used for extracting petroleum from the sea. This was going too far. He was setting up an oil rig for which he required the permission of the government, which I knew he hadn't taken.

Jazz had already started setting up the oil rig!

I learnt that the oil would be pumped into a pipeline which would run under the sea. This pipeline would run to just six kilometers across to the coast of the neighboring country. The neighboring country was run by a rogue military regime. The sea channel separating our country's remote island (where we were located) from the neighboring country was really shallow about three hundred feet deep. This meant that, no naval or commercial ships and submarines, would ever travel in this sea lane, barring few small boats. This would ensure that the sea bed pipeline will never be under any threat of detection or damage. The oil will then be smuggled out of the neighboring country's remote port via oil tankers across the world! This was plain stealing of national wealth!

This pipeline would run to just six kilometers across to the coast of the neighboring country.

Suddenly, I received a call from Wendy. 'Ryan, we need you here right now. Come quickly'.

I rushed back to the trio's computer workroom. Peter said, 'Ryan, Eye On is ready. By tomorrow evening it will be installed in all the corners of the island'. Aryan added, 'Yes, by tomorrow evening this island will be under surveillance. And, please don't forget that if Eye On finds any suspicious activity going on, it will start alerting. Although Smart Protection recognizes all people whose data is stored in it, yet if any identified person is caught doing any suspicious activity, it will send an alert signal'.

I got tensed. I didn't know what to do next. If *Eye On* spotted me doing anything suspicious, it would send the alert signals. I had no idea of what should be done next.

But, even if *Eye On* identified me, I had to go on with my mission. *Eye On* was a challenge for me.

The following week, was the week of action. I gathered all the people who were working there and also the constables who had agreed to come on my side. In the past few days, I had to face quite a few thrashings from the 'smuggler constables' as they were called. 'Smuggler Constables' was a separate group of constables. This group was a segregated one and the constables were contended with their jobs as henchmen, guarding an illegal business.

They had seen me staring at the sea through my binoculars and had threatened me that they would get me black listed.

All the chefs out there were very much into their jobs and bigheadedly called themselves as 'established smugglers'.

Amazingly, all people of the worker association came into my team, leaving aside the aged ones. It wasn't their fault that they had lost hope. They were sad and disappointed. I had taken some of the constables who had agreed to come to my team, including the constable who had given information to me in the beginning.

I narrated the plan to my team. They were amazed and readily agreed. I told each one their role in the mission. Everybody had the dedication to do it. We had to complete our goals, no matter how hard they seemed. And then, the Monday, of the following week, finally arrived. Our first mission was to get all the 'smuggler constables' and the chefs and give them a particular drug. This drug would get them all unconscious and pave way for the progress of our plan.

All the people were well rehearsed with their roles. Everyone had revised their parts. I was just hoping for the success of the plan. We had crossed our fingers and were hoping for the best. In our hearts and minds we had only one thing— 'In the name of the Father, the Son and the Holy Spirit . . . Amen' . . . the holy chant, which gives strength and hope to the soul.

Now all was in the hands of God. We only had the power to execute our plan.

CHAPTER 7
THE IMPLEMENTATION

Jacob, one of the helpers of the main chef, was the only person from the association of the chefs, who wanted liberty. Eventually I found a really good friend in him. I sent him to blend drugs in the constables' grub. Since Jacob was one of the helpers of the main chef, so nobody really had a doubt about his activities. He successfully blended the drugs and soon, all the constables fell asleep. The drug was very strong. The affected would sleep for about six to seven hours. In the next few hours, we had to complete our second step. But one problem was bothering us. Jacob had burnt his hand while mixing the drug. He had also dropped some drug powder and food on the floor.

While doing all this I suddenly remembered that Eye On was installed in all the rooms. The constables and chefs had had their food in their dining hall. When I went to that hall, all of them were lying unconscious. I had taken Wendy along with me. She knew very well how to detect if Eye On was installed in a particular place. She had a remote in her hand which she could use to detect Eye On's presence.

She pushed a red button on the remote and said 'Eye On, 2439416 Detection Mode on. This is Wendy. I repeat, Eye On 2439416 Detection Mode on.' Suddenly a robotic voice spoke up. 'Eye On cannot be detected in this area. Hi Wendy, Eye On has not been installed in this area. I would recommend that you install it as soon as possible.' Wendy replied, 'Okay thanks. I'll do the needful. Detection mode, shut down. I repeat, Detection Mode shut down.'

The remote went off. I called my teammates. I told Jacob to clean up the mess as quickly as possible. We had got sacks with us. We took all the people and put them into individual sacks. By the end of it, we had a total of fifty eight sacks. We escorted these sacks to a large room. This room had Eye On installed in it. We knew that Eye On would be present here, so we got the constables and chefs in sacks. Had we dragged them and got them to the room in an unconscious state, Eye On would've found it suspicious. So we opted for putting them into sacks.

The hall opened into a comparatively smaller cell. We loosened the cords of the sacks, pulled out the persons and left them on the floor. As for the sacks, we took them with us for future use. The only glitch was that the constables and chefs would come back to their senses in about six to seven hours. Subsequently they would try to come out from the main room also. Therefore, we decided that we would blend the drug in some food also. Whenever they would wake from sleep, they'll be puzzled to see themselves in a cell. Since we would've locked the cell, from outside, there would be no way for them to come out. They would keep trying and finally when they would feel tired, they would resort to having their meals.

But here too, we had a small conspiracy. I knew very well, that they would know what had been done previously with their food. Had the food been kept right in front of them, they would've known that it was again a trick being played on them. So, very cunningly, I told my teammates to keep the food in the small closed shelves in the cell. I also told them to keep some water. This way, it'd look more normal.

Such cells were common and food was usually kept in the shelves provided. The cells were primarily used for those people who were caught doing something which was against the rules of the island. Fortunately, at that time, most of the cells were empty. So we didn't face much difficulty in putting them into a cell, just big enough for those fifty eight people. Also the constables didn't really know as to which cell was empty, since they did not visit the cells frequently, although they had to. All said and done, they did not do their duties properly. So, they also didn't know that the food had been kept by us. Generally, empty cells did not have food. So, their ignorance was going to result in their defeat.

It was then time for my second step. I think God was with me at that time. My next step was to poison the Chief Advisor of Jazz. And at that very point of time, he came and told us to come for our supper . . . or rather morsels. But we were clever enough. I simply refused on everyone's behalf by saying 'We haven't worked as much to feel hungry.' At first, he was unwilling to consider my statement. 'Look, I do not know you but I'm not asking for your personal opinion. The other people have to have their supper. You are nobody to deny supper for them', he said. I said, 'Sir, I'm sorry if you felt insulted by my statement. Before you came, we were discussing the fact that none of us were feeling the pangs as we usually do after we work. I think that was because the work load was less today. We have been sitting in our rooms since three thirty in the afternoon. Usually, we work till half past six in the evening.' He asked fiercely, 'So, you mean to tell me that, since half past three you people have been sitting here and have still not felt hungry?' I replied, trying to keep my calm, 'Sir, we had some food from our respective cupboards. All of us had saved up some food for emergency. It happens sometimes, that we might feel really hungry, so we had kept some food separately for such times.' Finally, my answer convinced him. 'Okay, I'll leave then.' He walked away. I saw him in some distance and then he disappeared into the night. Suddenly, I remembered that he would go to surely go to the rooms of the constables and chefs. When he would not find anybody, he would come back to us.

I kept thinking and all of a sudden he came back and stood right in front of me. I hadn't thought of anything to say. I went completely blank, when I saw him.

'Where are all the constables and chefs?' he asked.' 'They all have gone for their meeting with the supreme attendant of our head', I replied, not knowing really what I was saying. 'I don't think that there was any meeting mentioned in the schedule.' I quickly used my brains and replied, 'Absolutely right sir! There was no meeting today, but the supreme attendant had sent across a message saying that he had to take a special meeting today.' And before he could say anything else, I decided to give him the temporarily poisoning victuals and make him snooze for some time. We served the food to him and he too dozed off.

We decided that, this much was enough for the day. I looked at my watch. It was half past seven sharp. We had given the drug to the constables and chefs at around quarter to seven. They would come back to their senses by around quarter to twelve. The Chief Advisor was also kept in the cell with the other constables and chefs. Luckily, we had the 'good constables' on our side, so I sent three of them to be on guard around the room. I was delighted by our progress. The 'bad' part of the Protection Squad was under my control, and the 'good' part was on my side. Nothing could be better!

Soon, the constables and chefs came back to their senses. But the guards were good at their work. The chefs and constables inside, kept struggling with the steel doors and the two jail strength windows of the room. I had to thank Jazz for one thing at that time. He had made the doors and windows so strong that it was impossible to break them open. The walls were made of concrete and the steel doors were of prison quality. Since, the after effects of the drug had not yet gone; the chefs and constables were rather weak and got tired quickly. After some time, the noise from inside subsided. They must've gone, had their food and dozed off again. This overdose was to keep them asleep for at least three days. It was enough time for me to complete my mission. In between we had decided to go slowly into the room and replace their food.

What I was worried about was my constant enemy—*Eye On*. It would've surely recorded their activity and would've kept it under the tag of suspicious behavior. By morning time, it would send the recording to the main computers. I approached Aryan and asked him for some assistance.

I said, 'Okay, Aryan I need some help. The constables and chefs are lying unconscious in the cell. A while ago, they had behaved in a peculiar and rebellious manner, since they wanted to come out of the main room. Eye On would've recorded that behavior. Now, it will send the recording to the main computers. I am afraid that we'll be caught. Is there a way to stop the recording from being sent to the main computers?' He replied, 'I can't promise to you but I'll try my best. I might have just received a copy of the recording on my computer. Let me check.'

He checked his computer. Yes, he had received a copy of the recording. He said, 'Ryan, you're really lucky. I just remembered that the first recordings were to come to our trio for approval; just to check if the recordings were done properly, or if *Eye On* required some modification.' So yes, I was indeed fortunate. We viewed the recording and saw those constables and chefs in their half-conscious state, banging the doors and windows. Soon they went back to the cell.

I asked Aryan, 'Well, so can you do something to stop this recording from going to the main computers?' He replied 'Well, I may be able to stop its transmission.' At that time Peter and Wendy came in.

Peter said, 'Hey Ryan, what's the matter? You look tensed . . .' Wendy added, 'Yeah, tensed for sure. What's happened?' I replied telling them what was bothering me. 'Aryan, weren't we told to review some minor recordings, if they came to us?' said Peter. Aryan replied, 'Oh . . . okay right. So, I can stop this recording from being sent.'

Wendy added, 'Ha ha . . . Ryan you are indeed very fortunate!' Four of us talked for a while and then I proceeded towards my room.

Emily and Graham were waiting for me. Graham said, 'Where were you? We haven't had supper till now.' Emily added, 'Yeah, you should be back in time. If some superintendent or advisor spots you roaming about the island at this time of the night, you'll be in trouble.' I said, 'Two of you needn't worry about me. I know very well how to handle this . . .' I did not finish. We had supper and talked for a while. Later, Emily and Graham went back to their respective rooms. I slept off thinking of the next day's plan.

Next day arrived. This day was the day of one of the most crucial jobs. We had to poison the supreme attendant of Jazz. The supreme attendant never visited the rooms or workplaces himself and so he was totally unaware of what was happening. If somebody had to speak to him, that person would first have to take an appointment.

Now, this was a special day for us. Fortunately, I got the appointment. I went and spoke to him in the following hour. I convinced him to come and see the workers once. I knew that he would start doubting me if he saw that the constables and chefs were absent. So, I told him to come through his secret tunnel passage. When he inquired why, I told him that the weather had been predicted to be very bad and everyone at work had been dismissed. And in reality also, the weather was turning bad. When he came at around half past four, the sky was much clouded and the day had gone almost dark. He came through the tunnel, which opened into the worker association's common sitting room. At last, he reached the room and to 'welcome' him I had made two ladies stand at the door with garlands of flowers. The flowers were venomous and could get riveted into the skin very rapidly.

Just as I heard his footsteps, I signaled to the ladies to get ready. 'Welcome sir, welcome.' 'Thank you.' 'Sir, here is a garland of the choicest flowers, just for you.' 'Thank you once again.' He came inside and the other people who had been assigned the task of tending to the superintendent, served starters to him. 'Well, well! I am astonished to see, that you have a hale and hearty supper ready. I had never thought of such fineness in these workers' mannerisms', he said, sardonically. 'Sir, it is the work of observation, that we have learnt how to behave with such intricacy in our mannerisms', I replied, trying my very best not to show my disgust. 'So, Ryan, I've seen your dedication towards this association. It is indeed laudable. Your efforts to call me here . . . something I've never really seen in any other person affiliated with the worker association', said the annoying imbecile. 'I am glad, Sir, that you think of me this way. But I would feel rather pleased, if you would also be acquainted with the commendable efforts of my partners. And Sir, I'm not from the worker association. I'm a geologist.' I said. 'Oh, okay. You're a geologist. That's interesting. And yes surely, your work for organizing this supper . . . your brain and the brawn of these workers!'

I began losing my cool and felt offended. Now and then, the statements made by the superintendent got my face suffused with anger, which was becoming clearly visible. I could not tolerate the insults being done to my fellows. I indicated that food be served. Once he had finished his meal, we led him towards the door connected to the tunnel.

The poison which was running in his blood because of the flowers had by then made its effect in his body. I put my foot ahead and the imprudent tripped and fell down. The fall acted as a catalyst for the poison's last effect. He must've felt a sudden shock in his body and said 'You rascals! You will have to pay for this misdeed of yours. I ensure you, that my death shall be avenged by this association!', and he died on the spot. 'Avenge his death?' What about the persecution done to all the people imprisoned there? This was indeed a sheer case of stratification. Only the lives of certain people mattered . . . others' were just ordinary base commodities. His statement 'The association will avenge my death', made me laugh. Who would avenge his death? When the bad society was trapped and the good society was united, no one could or would avenge his death.

CHAPTER 8
THE FINAL STEPS . . .

The third day arrived. My plan had been running quite smoothly. Yet, I was feeling as though something was wrong. At first I thought that it was the constables and chefs who were going to come to their senses. But then, I remembered that the food was being regularly replaced and the videos which were being recorded by *Eye On* were being sent to the trio. The trio was stopping their transmission. But *Eye On* was still bothering me. Wendy had told me that if the behavior of those fifty eight people in the cell continued in the same way, *Eye On* will identify it as 'Continuous Suspicion Creating Behavior'. It will then start sending the recordings to the main computers. She also told me that *Eye On* would start sending the recordings in three more days. The suspicion meter was increasing.

At around half past three in the afternoon, I heard someone murmuring in the common cabin. The common cabin was a medium sized hall, which had a few phones and fax machines. Anybody who wanted to contact the people from the authorities, he or she could fax or call up the offices.

I hate eavesdropping, but that day I had to. 'Yes, yes, I know exactly whatever happened to all the chefs and constables. Uh . . . yes sir, uh . . . mm . . . okay if you say so. I'll be sending the fax to you in another ten to fifteen minutes. Sure sir. Yes sir, you're welcome sir.' I understood the entire conspiracy. That boy on the telephone was one of my teammates, Harry. He was from the worker association. So the thing now was—a conspiracy against a conspiracy. That sounded interesting. But the thing that puzzled me was that, why would he betray us?

I kept standing there till the time he was inside, sending the fax. I saw him coming out and quickly hid behind the bush nearby. I decided to trail him. I followed him and reached the main building. The time was five minutes to four and the offices in the main building would close at quarter past four. He had exactly twenty minutes to do what he wanted to. He went inside the building. There was quite a commotion in the building. Everyone was engaged in their work. I followed him upstairs. The lobbies were mostly empty. Fortunately, I was dressed in something what I'll call as semi-formals. I was wearing a corduroy pant and a shirt from Armani, one of my most favorite shirts. Luckily, it was in my back pack.

Suddenly Harry stopped. He turned behind but thankfully, I slid behind long and flowing curtains of the lobby. I was surprised to see curtains of such a rich class of silk. But soon, I got back on my mission. I peeped outside and saw that Harry had left the lobby. I thought that I lost track of him and so I paced towards the end of the lobby. There were no turns beyond that. On my left was Jazz's cabin and on my right was his secretary's cabin. I noticed Jazz's secretary's name and I was astonished. It was Mr. Rupert K. He was the same person who had signed the agreement of the oil rig with Jazz. I walked away and went outside.

I went and called Jazz with one of the phones in the common cabin where many phones were kept to call any staff member. I got to know Jazz's number from John, my colleague, whom Jazz had also trapped. I called up and thought that if Jazz picked up the phone, I'd speak in a different voice.

I went and called Jazz with one of the phones in the common cabin where many phones were kept to call any staff member.

His secretary answered the phone. 'This is Mr. Rupert K. Is there something important to be done?' I got befuddled. Mr. Rupert K. was the business partner of Jazz. How could he have been his secretary? Why would Jazz use such a rich man as his secretary and then buy an oil rig from him? Suddenly something struck my mind. Mr. Rupert K. was Jazz's business partner and was pretending to be his secretary, so that both of them could supervise the work on the island. This way, no one would doubt on either of them.

Once again, he spoke. 'Hello, is there someone on the line?' I replied hastily. 'Yes, yes sir. I need an appointment with Mr. Jazz.' 'I cannot assign an appointment until you give me your name', he said. I replied, 'Yes, sure sir. I . . . I'm Troy.' I faked my identity or else, I would've got caught. He replied rather hastily, 'I'll be sending a fax to you within few hours for the confirmation of your appointment. Please keep checking the common cabin for your fax', he said. 'Thank you, sir', I replied. 'Sure', he said. That was the end of our conversation. I went back to my room.

I checked the time and noticed that it was half past five. I was enthralled and tired by my discoveries. Harry had ditched us and Rupert K.

was pretending to be Jazz's assistant. I decided to have my meal early and then sleep off to be fresh for the next day.

The next morning, I discussed my plan with Wendy, Aryan, Peter, Emily, Graham and the people of the worker association. It was decided that I would go to Jazz's cabin. I had to end the mission. Wendy spoke with Emily for the first time and so did Peter and Aryan with Graham. It was a good bonding for the five of them. I had gone to the common cabin for my fax. The time of my appointment was half past two in the afternoon. It was lunch time, but I had to go.

When I walked into the main building, I noticed all the offices. All the sub-superintendents, the superintendent, advisors and supervisors had their offices in the main building. When I reached Jazz's office, I took a deep breath and went inside. Nobody was present there. Then I assumed that he must have gone for his usual walk till the port. I went to the sliding glass window and saw him and Harry coming towards the main building. I had no idea of what I should have done. Before I could do anything, I heard their footsteps approaching the room. I rushed and hid behind the curtains. I tried to keep the sound of my breath as low as possible. The curtains were making it difficult for me to breathe. I was getting claustrophobic. He walked into the room and with his back facing me; he started glaring at the map of the sea route.

I rushed and hid behind the curtains.

He said to Harry, 'Harry, I'm thankful to you for telling me what has happened here. You've always been loyal to me. But, now since you know what my actual wish is, I think it's high time I should shut you down . . .' Harry's shoulders stooped. In a broken voice, he replied, 'Sir, I do not understand. I've been loyal to you; I'll be loyal to you in future also. Why would I leak any of your information? Please trust me sir!' 'How do I know that you'll be loyal to me in future? I think I should bid good bye to you', Jazz replied in a nasty way. Kaboom! He shot Harry. I heard him murmuring to himself, 'Ryan, you won't survive for long now.' He went outside. All the secrets which Harry held had gone away with him to another world. I opened all the drawers of Jazz's desk. I couldn't find anything much of use except a diary and a weird looking small machine. I kept the diary on the side table. I noticed something on the side table. It was a small chip. I took the chip and wondered what it could be used for. Suddenly, something struck my mind. I took the chip and tried fitting it into a small slit in the weird machine which I had found. Viola! It fit in. I pushed a blue button. A small needle enclosed in a glass case, which was fixed on the machine, started going round and round. I increased the volume and heard a conversation. I recognized that it was Jazz and Harry conversing. Harry started, 'Sir, it is Ryan Herman who is the root of all problems.' Jazz said angrily, 'Ryan Herman! I know him very well; he'll pay for whatever he's done. My business is on the verge of getting destroyed.' Harry said, 'I can understand Sir and having been your junior in school, I feel that I should support you, not them.' Jazz replied, 'You better do. Or else . . . ' He didn't finish. 'Sir, I am being with them to win their trust. I am supporting only you', Harry replied. Jazz just said, 'Hmph . . . okay, thank you Harry. You may leave.' The conversation stopped there. I wondered as to who could've recorded their conversation. I went back to Graham and Emily. They told me that all meetings of Jazz are recorded. He must've got a copy of the meeting and left it on the side table.

I looked at my watch. It was half past three. I knew that I had to end the mission that day itself. I had a light lunch and left for the main building again. I reached Jazz's cabin when suddenly, Mr. Rupert, Jazz's secretary cum business partner, called out my name. I turned behind. He had a revolver in his hand. He fired! Very quickly, I moved aside. He got confused for a moment. I ran towards him, but he fired again. The bullet just went like a tangent past my shoulder. Jazz must've shown him a photo of me and told him to shoot me down, if he spotted me alone at some point of time.

I was lucky enough to be saved from that shot. Before he could do anything else; I grabbed him by the collar and snatched the gun from his hand. He was frightened and surrendered immediately. I shot him. I did not feel guilty. I realized that a silencer had been attached to the gun. So, it didn't make the slightest noise.

I moved towards Jazz's cabin. I went inside. It was empty. I looked around the room. Once again, I heard footsteps approaching the cabin. Suddenly I heard Jazz's voice. He started wailing. 'No . . . no . . . no . . . Rupert! Not you now! Ryan, I'm coming for you.' I had to hide behind the curtains once again.

Curtains were my lucky charm. He entered the room and sat down on the sofa. I saw him through the curtains. He was sobbing. He said, 'I'm destroyed. Everything's gone. My business will go down now. All of it has been destroyed so rapidly. Why? What went wrong in my planning? I need the riches. I have to rule the world. Rya—Ryan! I'm coming for you. By tomorrow you will be finished. No one will be able to find your traces on this planet. Had I wished I could've come to your room and killed you there and then, but I wish to *finish* you . . . finish you! My work has come to a long halt. And now I'll halt you Ryan . . . Wait, what am I saying? I'll stop you, I'll finish you!'

Just at that moment, I came out. I saw him and felt sad for him, since he had been one of my closest friends. But then, his dreams were illicit; not permissible. I looked at him again and got enraged. I turned towards the door, and chuckled.

He turned his head and looked at me. Only my back was visible to him. He asked in a stern tone, 'Who are you and what are you doing here?' 'You are asking me, that who I am?' I replied, in a modulated voice. 'Yes, I am asking you that who you are', said Jazz, a bit scared. 'I am your end. I shall finish you.' 'What are you saying? Please be more candid. 'Just zip up!' I turned towards him and he was mystified. 'Ryan? How come you're here in my cabin?' The Protection Squad and the chefs are done for! They're all locked up and unconscious. And now it's your turn. You'll be the last now.' I said very angrily. 'You are my best friend, aren't you Ryan?' he pleaded. 'Oh, just zip up and stop calling me your best friend. I know your motives and your great wish to finish me and . . . Jazz; you're nothing more than my most familiar enemy now.'

My words and thoughts were coming out in front of him. I wanted to say a lot more, but I couldn't. I couldn't believe the situation I was in. I don't know why, but my mood suddenly turned pensive. Maybe that was because; I had to assassinate my best friend. I knew that I could not let a criminal like him survive; he was going psychic. He could kill many people in one go. He had the mind of a killer now. He knew just one thing—he had to kill me to get his business going.

But, at that point of time, I just knew that Jazz was right there in front of me and I was standing there like an imbecile. Completely dazed by whatever was happening, I leaped out of the window beside me. I fell on the coarse ground, but did not get injured, even after falling from such a height. Out of nowhere, Jacob came in front of me. 'Hey pal, get up! You have to end this mission of ours; no one else can!' He lent a hand and helped me to get up.

I got up and ran inside the building and towards Jazz's cabin. By then, Jazz had managed to escape by the back door of the main building. He was fast, very fast. He managed to come down from the cabin on the top floor, and ran outside through the back door, on the ground floor. I looked through the window and saw him in the distance, almost ready to board a ferry boat. I ran down again and went towards the sea. He saw me coming towards him and took out his revolver. Kaboom! The shot hit my right shoulder. I felt severely hurt and the pain gushed through my body. Yet, I managed to keep my legs stable and continued to run. I finally reached the sea. Jazz was standing right there in front of me. That was a face to face encounter. Both of us were taking deep breaths. I could see the rage in his eyes. But along with that rage, I could also see terror in his eyes. He started running once again. He approached the armoury. It was six in the evening. Nobody was present inside. *Eye On* was installed in the armoury too. It was present right on the door. Smart Protection recognized Jazz and opened the auto locking system. He got inside and I ran behind him. Now, there was no escape. There was only one window which was too small for him to escape. It was just a small space through the wall. Jazz had called his end by invitation.

Once again, I became thoughtful. There I was, standing in the most dangerous situation of my life. Either I could take up the opportunity to finish him there and then, or I could just turn into a prune once again and risk my life. I felt like I was placed on a guillotine . . . in absolute dilemma.

Suddenly I heard a slight creaking noise which was sharp enough to get me back to my sense of mission. Jazz was trying to take out a revolver from one of the drawers. I ran towards him, held his

**He approached the armoury. It was six in
the evening. Nobody was present inside.**

hand and nodded in an unwilling way. I was furious
and nervous too. Again, I thought that what I was
about to do was wrong. All the good memories I
shared with Jazz started playing in my mind like a
slide show. All the random memories flashed before
me like pictures. I could hear those conversations
which I had for long hours with him. All this

happened in such a short span of seconds that I was forced to think, over and again 'Killing a friend?! What is wrong with me?' But thankfully I did not bother about such thoughts for long and said to Jazz, 'Not this time buddy.'

CHAPTER 9

THE EVENT OF CONCLUSION . . . NEARLY

I slapped Jazz on the face. He got furious and punched me so hard that I fell down. But I got up and punched him. He fell down with a great thud. But that was not the end. He got up once more and grabbed my arm. He twisted it and pushed me towards the door. I turned very quickly and pulled out a drawer from the chest. I took out a revolver and kept it in my pocket. Suddenly, Jazz started hitting me with paper weights which led to bleeding, from the upper right part of my forehead. I hit him back with a stick kept in the large room. He began to limp. I took advantage of this and pushed him towards the wall. He hit his collar bone and fractured it. He tried to get up once more but luck was in my favor. I quickly took out my revolver and stood right in front of him. He had no way to escape. 'I am sorry friend, please don't do this. I shall give you an equal share in the businesses', he pleaded. 'Do not call me your friend. Although I'm a geologist, yet if I ever have to start a business, I have far better ideas of a good and legal business. You were always a cheater. During school exams, you cheated, while I resorted to being fair. When you wanted admission into an engineering college, you bribed the authorities. And when the time came to do something good in life, you decided to become the richest man in the world. And, to do that, you wanted to start a diamond mine. For that you set up a smuggling business to get money. You also set up an oil rig; doing nothing but stealing national wealth. I'm sure that you will export the oil for being sold in the black market. Say yes or no.' He didn't say anything. I asked again, 'Yes or no?' He started sobbing. He replied in a very low voice, 'Yes, yes. I did all of it.' I yelled at him, 'You're a cheater! You're a cheater.' Suddenly, a Protection Squad turned up out of nowhere. Eye On had sent information about the violent behavior in the ammunition center. I got very confused. I had trapped all of the Protection Squad and the good constables were working for me. What I couldn't understand was the origin of this new squad.

One of them said, 'You are under arrest. Mr. Jazz, you're safe now. We, the cops of the Clandestine Protection Squad are here to protect you, sir. We were in hiding, but now, our aim is to protect the master.' Jazz broke out in tears. He screamed and shouted. 'I don't need any protection! I have to pay for my deeds. I, Jazz Loner announce the freedom of all workers. Everybody has the liberty to go back from where they came. Thy might is greatest, oh Lord! I know I don't deserve a place in heaven. Send me to hell, oh Lord!' he said, very disgusted. He snatched the gun from my hand. Kaboom! He shot himself.

I stood there aghast. I couldn't believe that Jazz had slain himself. I fell down on my knees. I was twenty five years old and so was Jazz. I had befriended him as a child when we both were around eight years old. Seventeen years of friendship had ended. I was broken and started crying. Why did he do all of that? What got the feeling of greed in him? How could he have been so cruel to torture people and make them work by hitting and torturing them? Why?

All I knew was that those answers had all gone away with him. And those answers wouldn't have made any relevance. He had committed too many crimes to be forgiven. The people of the Protection Squad had left by then. Suddenly I heard the trio and EmiGram. I had named Emily and Graham as EmiGram, to make things easier for me. I called out to them. They came in and saw Jazz dead. I told them about whatever had happened. They consoled me. At last I got over the death of Jazz, and took it as his fault.

Everyone was overjoyed to see Jazz dead. And later, so was I. I had destroyed evil from one part of the world.

The news of Jazz's death spread like wildfire. All the people came running towards me when they heard the news. I waved to them with a bright and wide smile on my face, though my eyes were still soggy.

While everyone partied and cheered that night, I went to Jazz's cabin. I picked up the diary which I had found earlier. Unbuttoning the diary, I flipped through the pages. I came upon a page which caught my attention. It read:

Dear Diary,

'Ryan, my best friend . . . I ditched him and I know he'll be devastated. But it was important to do so. He's a clever person. He can be a threat to me. If he had found out about my businesses, he would've informed the authorities. So, I decided to destroy him emotionally and make him work in my business on the island. In this fashion, he would not be able to do anything. I know Ryan very well. He is an emotionally weak and sensitive person and gets swayed away by a few sweet words and kind gestures. He's incapable of bearing the burden of working on the island. He'll be destroyed

mentally after being deceived by me. But, this is for the good.

You know, as a kid, my parents were murdered because they were under debt. They were unable to repay the huge amount of loan to the moneylender, who was a very, very rich man. He was too powerful and ruthless. My parents asked him for an extension in the duration, but he refused. They were unable to repay the loan. The moneylender threatened to get them murdered. He had started getting my parents beaten with whips. My parents decided to approach the court for help, since physical manhandling for the reason of inability to repay the loan, was not justified.

They were under debt, so, the court sided with the moneylender and my parents lost the case. It was sheer injustice. The moneylender was enraged because my parents had spoken against him. He got them murdered and snatched

*the only property we had, our small
cottage. Thereafter, my aunt took up the
responsibility of raising me. But, she too
was only interested in some of the money
which was mentioned in my parents' will.*

*From that time onwards, I understood
the importance of money. And today, I'm
on the verge of becoming the richest man in
the world! No one can stop me.'*

Goodnight

Jazz.

Jazz had become blind in his rage and greed.
But I feel that whatever had happened was for the
good.

The next day I went to the nearest public
telephone booth and called the police. The police
investigated the area and took our statements. We
all were set free. I gave the password of the PIST to
the police for some information they would need.
When I had taken the password from the trio, I
had tracked down some of the transactions which

were going on. I had then made a note of the people involved. I had also blocked some of the transactions from moving further. Each time a transaction would come, it would be sent back with an error message.

In this way, I had at least got control over the transactions and halted them. Those people involved in the transactions were also arrested.

The constables and chefs, who were still lying unconscious in the cell, were arrested as they were proven guilty. All the arrestees were escorted to the prison in the city, far away from the island. We all were taken to the nearest city via a ship. Everyone bid goodbye and dispersed.

All this while, I had never realized that I had fallen in love with Wendy. Fortunately, her mother was thankful enough to ask me if she could do something for me in the happiness of seeing her daughter return. I asked her hesitantly if I could marry her daughter. She said, 'Well, that isn't my decision. Wendy's always been a person of independent choices. If she wishes, then yes, you both can surely go ahead.' Wendy came in at that moment. She held my hand, and said, 'Mum, Ryan is mine and I want to… marry him! Well, I know it's okay with you, so I am not going to ask you.' 'Look, I told you, didn't I Ryan? Go boy, your wish has come true!' Wendy's mum said in an enthusiastic tone.

I had to go for Jazz's cremation, as I had become nostalgic. While he was being carried to the grave, I noticed a laceration near his collar bone, which had been left during the tussle in the ammunition room.

The wedding ceremony took place some days later. One day, Wendy and I were walking down the market street when we met Aryan and Peter. We spoke for a while and then bid goodbye. We laughed a lot and Wendy whispered to me, 'Ryan, I had never imagined that I'll meet you on the island. Thank God that I went there.' I was overjoyed and said to her, 'I'll never, ever leave you. You'll have to stay with me till the end. And, I mean it.' We went back to our homes after a while. My life had become heaven. I was living very comfortably. Sometime later, I got the President's bravery award.

CHAPTER 10

BAFFLED UP

O n 16th September, Wendy conceived our first kid. It was a baby boy. I was suddenly reminded of the fact that Jazz too, was born on the same date. But then, I thought that it was a mere coincidence. We named our boy as Talyessin.

We brought him up with utter care and cautiousness. We didn't want our past to affect him in any way. Any possible memories of Jazz and the island in the form of written notes or photographs were removed from the house.

It was Talyessin's fifth birthday. We celebrated it and called on some of our neighbors for the occasion. The next day, Wendy went to her office, while I stayed back at home, on a leave from work. At around four thirty in the afternoon, Talyessin came to me and sat beside me as I was reading the newspaper. He said, 'Dad, I don't know why, but last night, I dreamt of a very strange island. I saw a room on which the letters J and Z were faintly visible to me. The next moment someone started fighting with me and then I felt pain gushing through my head, as though a bullet had passed through it. Along with this, I also saw many poor people working. It was a very strange dream indeed, dad. And when I thought for some time about the dream, I felt like someone was whispering into my ear. The person said to me, "You're a cheater. You're a cheater".

I was astonished. I called him closer and asked him about anything else which he knew. He said, 'Dad, since the time I've got that dream, I've been feeling a strong connection with islands and caves. And I feel oddly guilty, although I haven't done anything.'

I told him to go and be in his room. I began to think about what Talyessin had said to me. I had come across the phenomena of rebirth, revival and life after death, while reading about oriental religions and beliefs. But was all of that true?

I felt pain gushing through my head, as though a bullet had passed through it

**I was dumbstruck on listening to
what Talyessin had just said.**

Did Talyessin just overhear Wendy and my conversations? Was he just sharp enough to hear and reproduce facts in a manipulative manner? Or was it really a rebirth?

Suddenly my phone started ringing. It was Wendy. 'Ryan, I'll be coming home late tonight. I'll be home only by half past one in the morning. Is that alright with you?' I was completely lost in my thoughts, and didn't reply. 'Ryan, are you listening? I'll be home only by half past one in the morning'. I got surprised and returned to the conversation.

I replied, 'Yes, sure, I'm fine with it. See you then Wendy . . .' 'Okay then, bye Ryan.' She kept the phone down.

Soon, it was time for Talyessin to go to bed. I got his dinner ready, the ideal bowl of muesli with two sausages. I fed him and got him to change his clothes. Before he went to sleep I gave him his share of Galaxy, his favorite chocolate. While I made him put on his night suit, I noticed a faint scar on the skin above the collar bone. It was just the same scar as Jazz had got after the tussle in the ammunition room.

I almost fainted. All this was painting a hazy picture of Jazz in my mind. I jerked my head hard. I lifted up Talyessin in my arms, gave him a goodnight kiss on the forehead and laid him down on the bed. I was about to switch off the lights, when Talyessin asked me in a low voice, 'Dad, I'm not a cheater, right?' I didn't expect such a question. I replied, calming him down, 'No son, you're not. You're my son. And Ryan's son can never be a cheater'. He smiled and I turned off the lights and went to my room.

I kept thinking and looked at my watch. It was half past nine. Wendy was to return at half past one. I couldn't even think of telling Wendy of whatever I had heard from Talyessin or seen on his skin. She had completely moved on. But if Talyessin talked to her about Jazz or the caves or the island, she would get much tensed. But I couldn't stop that from happening. If it was to happen, it would happen.

It's been five days since the time Talyessin has not spoken directly about Jazz or anything of that sort. But he sure seems lost. Yesterday, Wendy asked him to have his glass of milk. Instead of coming to the kitchen, he went to the garden and sat there looking at a small setting of rocks which was in the shape of a cave. He kept glaring at it for half an hour, after which Wendy came and took him inside. When she told me about his weird behavior, I freaked out. She didn't understand my tension and put me off saying that I didn't understand the curiosity of kids. Should I tell her? Should I refresh the memories we had? I have no clue of what to do.

Is Talyessin really a body with Jazz's spirit? But my faith doesn't state rebirth.

But, by the slightest possibility, if Talyessin's statements are true, then I have to bring up another Jazz, in this world.